So Late in the Day

So Late in the Day

CLAIRE KEEGAN

faber

First published in 2023
by Faber & Faber Ltd
The Bindery, 51 Hatton Garden
London ECIN 8HN

Typeset by Faber & Faber Ltd
Printed in the UK by CPI Group (UK) Ltd, Croydon CRO 4YY

*This is a work of fiction. All of the characters, organisations and events
portrayed in this novel are either products of the author's imagination
or are used fictitiously*

A CIP record for this book
is available from the British Library

ISBN 978-0-571-38201-9

2 4 6 8 10 9 7 5 3

For Loretta Kinsella

It stands plain as a wardrobe, what we know,
Have always known, know that we can't escape,
Yet can't accept. One side will have to go.

'Aubade' by Philip Larkin

So Late in the Day

1

On Friday, July 29th, Dublin got the weather that was forecast. All morning, a brazen sun shone across Merrion Square, reaching onto Cathal's desk where he was stationed by the open window. A taste of cut grass blew in and every now and then a close breeze stirred the ivy, on the ledge. When a shadow crossed, he looked out; a gulp of swallows skirmishing, high up, in camaraderie. Down on the lawns, some people were out sunbathing and there were children, and beds plump with flowers; so much of life carrying smoothly on, despite the tangle of human upsets and the knowledge of how everything must end.

Already, the day felt long. When Cathal looked again, at the top of the screen, it read 14:27. He wished, now, that he had gone out at lunchtime and walked as far as the canal. He could have sat on one of the benches there for a while and watched the mute swans and cygnets gobbling up the crusts and other scraps people threw down there, on the water. Without meaning to, he closed the budget distribution file he'd been working on before saving it. A flash of something not unlike contempt charged through him then, and he got up and walked down the corridor, as far as the men's room, where there was no one, and pushed into a stall. For a while he sat on the lid, looking at the back of the door, on which nothing was written or scrawled, until he felt a bit steadier. Then he went to the basin and splashed water on his face, and slowly dried his face and hands on the paper towel which fed, automatically, from the dispenser.

On the way back to his desk, he stopped for a coffee, pressed the Americano option on the machine, and waited for it to spill down, into the cup.

It was almost ready when Cynthia, the brightly dressed woman from accounts, came in, laughing on her mobile. She paused when she saw him, and soon hung up.

'All right there, Cathal?'

'Yeah,' he said. 'Grand. You?'

'Grand.' She smiled. 'Thanks for asking.'

He took up the coffee, leaving before he'd sugared it, before she could say anything more.

When he got back to his desk and looked at the top of the screen, it was 14:54. He was just reopening the file and reading over what was there and was about to compose some of the changes he would again have to make, when the boss stopped by.

The boss was a Northern man, a good ten years younger than himself, who wore designer suits and played squash at the weekends.

'Well, Cathal. How are things?'

'Good, thanks.'

'Did you get a bite of lunch, something to eat?'

'Yeah,' Cathal said. 'No bother.'

The boss was looking him over, taking in the usual jacket, shirt, tie and trousers, his unpolished shoes.

'You know there's no need to stay on,' the boss said. 'Why don't you call it a day?' He flushed a little then, seeming uneasy over the well-intentioned phrase.

'I'm just finishing the budget outline now,' Cathal said. 'I'd like to get this much done.'

'Fair enough,' the boss said. 'Whatever. Take her handy.'

The boss withdrew then, to his office, and

Cathal heard the door softly closing.

When he looked back out, the sky was blank and blue. He took a sip of the bitter coffee and stared again at the file he hadn't saved. It wasn't easy to see it now, in the glare of the sunlight, so he changed the font to bold and tilted the screen. For a while he tried again to focus on what was there, but in the end decided to settle down to the raft of letters which would all be identical, except for the name:

Dear ____ ,

Thank you for your application for a Bursary in Visual Arts. The selection committee has now convened, and made its decisions. The final round was extremely competitive, and we regret to inform you that on this occasion . . .

By 5 p.m., he had most of the rejections printed on letterhead and was waiting on the landing, for the lift. When he heard someone coming, he pushed through a door, to the stairwell. It was hotter and smelled musty there. The Polish girl who cleaned after hours was leaning against the banister, texting. He felt her watching him as he passed, and was glad to reach the foot of the stairs and the exit, to get out onto the street, where it was noisy and a hot queue of cars pushed at the traffic lights.

He took his tie off and felt in his jacket for the bus pass, which was there, in his breast pocket, and walked to the Davenport to wait for the Arklow bus. For no particular reason, a part of him doubted that the bus would come that day, but it soon came up Westland Row and pulled in unceremoniously and let the passengers on.

Almost every seat was occupied, and he had to take an aisle seat beside an overweight woman who slid a bit closer to the window to give him room.

'Wasn't that some day,' she said, brightly.

'Yeah,' Cathal said.

'They say it's meant to last,' she said. 'This fine weather.'

He had chosen badly; this woman would want to talk. He wished she would stay quiet – then caught himself.

'That's good to know,' he said.

'We're taking the grandkids to Brittas for a dip on Sunday,' she went on. 'If we don't soon go, the summer could get away on us. Don't the days fly.'

She took a tube of Polo mints from her pocket and offered him one, which he refused.

'How about you?' she said. 'Any plans for the long weekend?'

'I'm just going to take it easy,' Cathal said, threading the speech into a corner, where it might go no further.

He would ordinarily have taken out his mobile

then, to check his messages, but found he wasn't ready – then wondered if anyone ever was ready for what was difficult or painful.

'And we're taking them to my brother's dairy farm,' the woman went on. 'We don't want them growing up thinking milk comes out of a carton. Aren't children so privileged nowadays.'

'I suppose they are.'

'Have you children yourself?'

Cathal shook his head. 'No.'

'Ah, you could be as well off,' she said. 'They break your heart.'

He thought she would go on, but she reached into her bag and took out a book, *The Woman Who Walked Into Doors*, and was soon turning the pages, engrossed.

The traffic was heavier than usual at that hour, heading out of town and along the top of the N11, but when they'd passed the turnoff for Bray and got on the motorway, the road opened up. He looked out at the trees and fields sliding past, and the wooded hills beyond, which he noticed almost daily but had never climbed. Sooner than he'd expected, they were bypassing the turnoff for Wicklow Town and heading farther south, at much the usual time.

It had been an uneventful day and much the same as any other. Then, at the stop for Jack White's Inn, a young woman came down the aisle and sat in the vacated seat across from him. He sat breathing in her scent until it occurred to him that there must be thousands if not hundreds of thousands of women who smelled the same.

2

Little more than a year ago, Cathal had almost run down the stairwell from the office to meet Sabine, at the entrance to Merrion Square where the statue of Wilde lay against a rock. She was wearing a white trouser suit and sandals, sunglasses, a string of multicoloured beads around her neck. They'd crossed over to the National Gallery, to see the Vermeer exhibition; she'd paid for the tickets online. He had stood in close, breathing in her perfume, as they viewed the paintings. Although she admired Vermeer's women, most, to him, looked idle: sitting around, as though waiting for somebody or something that might never come – or staring at themselves in a looking glass. Even the hefty milkmaid seemed to be pouring the milk out at her leisure, as though she had nothing else or better to do.

They'd taken the bus down to his place in Arklow afterwards and lain in bed with the window wide open: a warm breeze and the steely sounds of his neighbour's wind chimes coming in, crossing the room. She had slept for an hour or more before walking to Tesco's for groceries, and making dinner: chicken roasted with branches of thyme, garlic and courgettes. The woman could cook; even now, he had to say that much for her. But a part of him always resented the number of dirty dishes, having to rinse them all before stacking them in the dishwasher – except for the roasting dish which she usually said they could leave to soak overnight, and was sometimes still there in the sink when he got back from work on Mondays.

They had met more than two years ago, at a conference in Toulouse. She was petite and brown-haired with a good figure and green eyes which were not quite properly aligned, a little bit crossed. He'd been drawn to how she was dressed: in a skirt and blouse of slate blue, how she seemed at ease in herself but alert to what was around her. He'd sat behind her on that first morning, and while the introductory speaker jargoned on, he'd looked at the little buttons on the back of her blouse, wondering if she'd fastened them through the loops by herself. There was no ring on her finger. He'd approached her at the coffee break and it turned out that she, too, worked in Dublin City Centre, for the Hugh Lane Gallery, and was renting a flat in Rathgar, which she shared with three postgraduates, younger women.

'Have you spent any time in Wicklow?'

'I've seen Glendalough and Avondale,' she'd

said. 'And walked the hills. It is such pretty countryside.'

'You might come down and take in some more of the countryside,' Cathal had said, and got her number, adding that they might have a drink after work one evening.

Things were lukewarm on her side at the beginning, but he didn't push. Then she started coming down on weekends, and staying over. She had grown up in Normandy, near the coast, and liked getting out of the city, liked the town of Arklow with the river running through it, the second-hand bookshop and the nearby beach where she often walked the strand barefoot, even in winter. Her father was French, had married an English woman – but her parents divorced when she was a teenager, and hadn't spoken since.

And then, at some point, Sabine began spending most of her weekends in Arklow, and they started going to the farmers' market on Saturday mornings. She didn't seem to mind the expense, and bought freely: loaves of sourdough bread, organic fruit and vegetables, plaice and sole and mussels off the fish van, which came up from Kilmore Quay. Once, he'd seen her pay four euros for an ordinary-looking head of cabbage. In September, she went out along the back roads with his colander, picking hazelnuts off the trees. Then a local farmer told her she could gather the wild mushrooms off his fields. She'd made hazelnut biscuits, mushroom soup. Almost everything she brought home she cooked with apparent light-handedness and ease, with what Cathal took to be love.

One afternoon, as they were walking past Lidl, she wanted to stop and buy cherries to make a tart but didn't have her purse. Cathal had said it was all right, that he would pay. She'd taken a metal scoop and weighed out a half kilo which, when they reached the cashier, came to more than six euros. When they got home, she washed then halved and stoned them at the kitchen island and drank a glass of the Beaujolais she'd brought down, and made the tart, a clafoutis, she called it. The pastry had to be left to chill while she made a custard. Then she rolled the pastry out with a cold wine bottle and fluted the edges deftly, with her thumbs.

Finally, when the tart was in the oven, he'd looked at their empty glasses and replenished them with the Beaujolais, and asked if they should marry.

'Why don't we marry?'

'Why don't we?' She'd let out a sound, a type of choked laughter. 'What sort of way is this of asking? It seems like you are almost making some type of argument against it.' She had just washed the flour off her hands at the sink, was drying them on the paper towel.

'I didn't mean it that way,' Cathal said.

'So what is it then, that you did mean?'

Her command of the English language sometimes grated.

'It's just something to consider, is all.' Cathal said. 'Won't you think about it?'

'Think about what, exactly?'

'About making a life, a home, here with me. There's no reason why you shouldn't live here instead of paying rent. You like it here – and you know neither one of us is getting any younger.'

She was looking at him, one eye looking directly into his and the other's gaze a little off, to one side.

'And there's no reason why we couldn't have a child,' he said, 'if you wanted.'

He'd watched her closely; she didn't seem to turn away.

'You like that idea?' Cathal asked.

'A child is not an idea,' she retorted.

'And we could get a cat,' he said quickly. 'You'd like a cat, I know.'

She'd let out a genuine laugh then, and Cathal felt some of her resistance subsiding and closed his arms around her – but it took more than three weeks and some persuasion on his part before she finally relented, and said yes. And then another two months passed before she found an engagement ring to suit her, at a fancy jeweller's off Grafton Street: an antique with one diamond set on a red-gold band, but it was loose on her finger, and had to be resized.

When they had gone back to collect it, some weeks later, on a Friday evening, an additional charge of 128 euros plus VAT was added for the resizing. He had taken her outside to the street then, saying they should refuse to pay this extra charge – but she'd insisted that they'd been told of the additional cost, and refused to say she had ever believed otherwise.

'Do you think I'm made of money?' he'd said – and immediately felt the long shadow of his father's language crossing over his life, on what should have been a good day, if not one of his happiest.

She had stared at him and was about to turn and walk, but Cathal backed down, and had apologised.

'Please wait,' he'd pleaded. 'I didn't mean it. I just didn't want to be taken advantage of, is all. I got it all wrong.'

He had gone back into the shop then and, with some difficulty, as his hands weren't steady, had prised the Mastercard from his wallet.

The jeweller, a white-haired man with gold-rimmed glasses, placed the ring into a little domed box, and handed him the card reader.

'You know that this item is non-refundable now, that it's custom-made and cannot be returned?'

'There'll be no need for anything like that,' Cathal said.

The jeweller pressed his lips together as though resisting an urge to say something more, but when the transaction was approved, he simply handed Cathal the receipt and the little box which weighed no more than a box of matches.

'Congratulations,' the jeweller said. 'May you have a long and happy marriage.'

They had gone to Neary's on Chatham Street afterwards, where it was quiet, and ordered tea and grilled cheese sandwiches, which the barman brought to their little marble-topped table. She had reached for the sugar, the ring catching the light, shining freshly on her hand, where he had placed it – but she had little appetite; took just a few bites out of the sandwich and let her second cup of tea grow cold.

A drizzle of rain started coming down as they walked past St Stephen's Green, to the bus stop. For almost half an hour they waited there, outside the Davenport, before the bus finally came, but the rest of the weekend went remarkably well: as the hours passed she seemed to slowly forgive him, to soften, and the time between them grew sweet again, perhaps even a little sweeter than it had ever gone, that hurdle of their first argument having been crossed.

3

When the bus stopped in Arklow, Cathal got off, along with some others. A big man in work clothes and wellington boots was sitting on the low wall outside the newsagent's licking an ice-cream cone, a 99. He nodded but did not speak – and Cathal wondered if this wasn't the farmer who'd told Sabine she could gather the mushrooms off his fields.

Cathal wasn't sure he would make it back to the house without meeting others and was relieved to reach his front door, where a bunch of wilted flowers lay. He stepped over them, turned the key in the lock, and pushed the door. A small pile of post had gathered inside, on the mat. He stooped to lift the envelopes and placed them on the hallstand, alongside the rest.

As soon as he had the door closed, he felt the house unusually still, and quiet. He stood for a minute and called out to Mathilde, the cat. When he called again and still there was no sound, his heart lurched and he went looking, opening doors, but the cat was nowhere to be found – until he found her, in the bathroom. He must have locked her in there, by mistake, before he'd left for work. He unlocked the back door and let her out, then opened the fridge.

There was nothing fresh there: a jar of three-fruits marmalade, Dijon mustard, ketchup and mayonnaise, champagne, a packet of short-dated rashers, a phallus-shaped cake with flesh-coloured icing which his brother had ordered, as a joke, for the stag party. He took a Weight Watchers chicken & veg out of the freezer and stabbed the plastic a few times with a steak knife before putting it into the microwave on high for nine minutes. Then he emptied the last pouch of Whiskas into the cat's dish, and filled the water bowl. As the bowl filled, a thirst came over him and he dipped his head and drank from the running tap. A feeling not unlike happiness momentarily crossed over his lips then, and down his throat. It was something he used to do in college: drinking from the water fountain at UCD after cycling in from the Stillorgan flat he shared with his brother and two other fellows – but he was so much younger then.

In the sitting room, he took his shoes off and picked up the remote. There was little of interest on: a rerun of the Wimbledon final, *Dr. Phil*, *Judge Judy*, a cookery programme with a man in chef's whites cutting an avocado in two and removing the stone, its skin, mashing its flesh up with a fork.

He opened the window wide and looked out at the street, at the brightness of the houses across the way. This evening, a bunch of helium balloons was tied to a gate and there were children bouncing on an inflated castle. He drew the curtains together, closing out the laughter, the light, and instantly felt a little better. He told himself that he should take a shower and change, but he did not feel like going upstairs, or changing. He slipped his belt off and pushed all the cushions to one side of the couch, and punched them together. There was no need for all those cushions; six of them, on one couch.

When the microwave dinged, he sifted through the channels again. Still there was nothing there he wanted to see, so he went back to the kitchen and took the tray out of the microwave, peeled off the cellophane. He sat at the island for a while with a fork, chewing and swallowing. Weight

Watchers. That had been her big thing since the first of April, so she wouldn't fit so snugly into the little vintage dress she'd found: a white lacy dress with pearls stitched here and there, onto the bodice. She hadn't minded showing it to him, was not superstitious. She'd stopped making dinner most evenings, except for the green salad with a vinaigrette which she usually made. He'd told her that it didn't matter, that she wasn't fat – but she wouldn't listen. That was part of the trouble: the fact that she would not listen, and wanted to do a good half of things her own way.

And then, this time last month, the moving van arrived with all of her possessions: a desk and chair, a bookshelf, boxes of books and DVDs, CDs, two suitcases filled with clothes, a large Matisse print of a cat with its paw in a fish tank, and some framed photographs of people he did not know – which she placed and hung about the house, pushing things back, as though the house now belonged to her also. A good half of her books were in French, and she looked different without her make-up, going around in a tracksuit, sweating and lifting things and making him lift and move his own things, pushing back furniture, the strain showing so clearly on her face. And there were pots and pans, a yoga mat, skirts and blouses, wooden hangers, a water filter, canisters of tea, a coffee grinder.

'Do you love me?' she asked, once most of her things were in place and several of his had been repositioned.

She had sat down beside him at that point, on the edge of the bed.

'Of course.'

'So what is wrong?'

'There's nothing.'

'Tell me.' She had insisted.

'I just don't know about this stuff, that's all.'

'Which stuff? My stuff?'

'These things. All your things. All this.' He was looking around: at the blue throw, the two extra pillows, pairs of shoes and sandals, most of which he'd never seen her wearing, poking out from under his chest of drawers.

He himself owned Nikes and just one pair of shoes.

'Did you think I would come with nothing?'

'It's just a lot.' He'd tried to explain.

'A lot? I do not have so very much.'

'Just a lot to deal with.'

'What did you imagine?'

'I don't know,' he said. 'Not this. Just not this.'

'I cannot understand,' she told him. 'You knew I had to leave the flat in Rathgar by the end of the month. You asked me to come here, to marry you.'

'I just didn't think it would be like this, is all,' he said. 'I just thought about your being here and having dinner, waking up with you. Maybe it's just too much reality.'

He made an attempt to pull her to him then so he would not see what was in her eyes, to block it out – but she was rigid in his arms and got up, determined to empty out the last box, pushing his razor and toothpaste to one side on the little glass shelf in the en suite, to make room for her own. And there were lotions, hair conditioner, contraceptives and a make-up bag, tampons.

She took a long shower then and changed and drank a full litre of Evian over a Chinese which he'd had to order, over the phone. The restaurant charged four euros for delivery. He'd wanted to walk down to collect it – it wasn't far – but she didn't feel like walking anywhere that night, and for some reason he did not want to leave her there, on her own.

After they'd eaten, a change seemed to come over her and she opened up a bit, and started to talk.

'I went out for a drink with one of your colleagues this week,' she began.

'Oh?'

'Yes,' she said. 'Cynthia took me to the Shelbourne.'

'I didn't know that you two knew each other.'

'We don't, really,' she said. 'She just handles the funding for some of our work at the gallery. In any case, we wound up sharing a bottle of Chablis, and started talking about men, Irish men – and I asked her what it is you really want from us, what is her experience.'

Cathal felt a sudden need to get up, but made himself stay in the chair, facing her.

'Would you like to know what she said?'

'I'm not sure.' He almost laughed.

'Then perhaps you can answer?'

'I don't know,' he said, truthfully. 'I've never once thought about it.'

'But am I not asking you to think about it now?'

He lifted his hand and reached for her plate, rose, and put her plate on the draining board under his own before leaning back and holding on to the ledge of the counter.

'I really don't know,' he said. 'What did she say?'

'She said things may now be changing, but that a good half of men your age just want us to shut up and give you what you want, that you're spoiled and turn contemptible when things don't go your way.'

'Is that so?'

He wanted to deny it, but it felt uncomfortably close to a truth he had not once considered. It occurred to him that he would not have minded her shutting up right then, and giving him what he wanted. He felt the possibility of making a joke, of defusing what had come between them, but couldn't think of anything – and then the moment passed and she turned her head away. That was the problem with women falling out of love; the veil of romance fell away from their eyes, and they looked in and could read you.

But this one didn't stop there.

'She also said that to some of you, we are just cunts,' she went on, 'that she often hears Irish men referring to women in this way, and calling us whores and bitches. We had reached the end of the bottle and had not yet eaten but I remember clearly – that's what she said.'

'Ah, that's just the way we talk here,' Cathal said. 'It's just an Irish thing and means nothing half the time.'

'Monika, the Polish cleaner, told her you were the only person in the whole building who didn't give her so much as a card at Christmastime. Is this true?'

'I don't know.' He genuinely didn't. He couldn't remember giving her something or not giving her anything.

'Do you know you've never even thanked me for one dinner I have made here, or bought any groceries – or made even one breakfast for me?'

'Did I not order your dinner tonight and pay for it? Did I not buy all those cherries for your fancy tart? And haven't I helped you here all day, moving all your stuff?'

'Did you help – or just watch?' she asked. 'And that night you bought the cherries at Lidl, you told me they cost more than six euros.'

'So?'

'You know what is at the heart of misogyny? When it comes down to it?'

'So I'm a misogynist now?'

'It's simply about not giving,' she said. 'Whether it's believing you should not give us the vote or not give help with the dishes – it's all clitched onto the same wagon.'

'Hitched,' Cathal said.

'What?'

'It's not "clitched",' he said. 'It's "hitched".'

'You see?' she said. 'Is not this just more of it? You knew exactly what I meant – but you cannot even give me this much.'

He had looked at her then and again saw something ugly about himself reflected back at him, in her gaze.

'Can you not even understand what I am talking about?' She seemed to be genuinely asking, looking not for an argument but an answer.

But Cathal didn't say much more. At least he didn't think he had said much more. He might, when things got heated, have made an ugly remark about her eyes – but he did not like to think of this. The fact was that he couldn't remember much else about that evening, except that he was glad he didn't have to help with any dishes afterwards; he'd simply put his foot down on the pedal of the bin and thrown the cartons from the Chinese on top of the other waste that had already accumulated there, before letting the lid drop.

4

It was past 8 p.m. when Cathal went back into the sitting room. He'd decided to watch a series on Netflix, to binge-watch another over the weekend, but a documentary had come on, on Channel 4, about Lady Diana, some type of commemoration, or an anniversary. He'd never held any interest in the Royal Family and yet found himself sitting in a type of trance: there she was, in the white, crumpled dress, with a veil over her face, getting out of the horse-drawn carriage with her father and turning to wave at the crowd before climbing the steps and taking the long walk up the aisle to marry the man waiting for her there, at the altar.

As soon as the vows were made and the wedding rings had been exchanged, Cathal automatically pressed the rewind button on the remote before realising it was not something he could rewind. And then Mathilde came in – he felt her coming back – and soon after, during the ads, the screen grew a bit fuzzy and his eyes stung.

He felt hot and took his socks off and dropped them on the floor and left them there. There was such pleasure in doing this that he wanted to do it again. Instead, he sat watching the second half of the programme with Diana getting pregnant and producing a son, and then another. Towards the end, after she had left her husband and had gone off with another man, a wealthy Egyptian, she was sitting out in a bathing suit in the sun, on a diving board. And then there was the car crash in the tunnel in Paris followed by her young sons following the hearse, and all those flowers rotting outside of Buckingham Palace and Kensington.

When the credits started to roll, he felt the need for something sweet, and went back into the kitchen. He opened the fridge and reached in for the flesh-coloured cake, lifted it out onto the island. He took the steak knife he'd used to pierce the cellophane of her Weight Watchers, and sliced the whole tip off. Then he took out the champagne and removed the foil and untwisted its wire cage. The bottle had been in there since the night of the hen party, as she had no taste for fizzy drinks. The cork was stubborn and tight – but he kept pushing at it with his thumbs until the cork gave and finally came away with an exhausted little pop.

Back in the sitting room, he sifted through the channels. Again, there was nothing there he really wanted to see. He swallowed mouthfuls of the cake and drank the champagne neither slowly nor in any rush until the cake and the champagne were gone, and then a painful wave of something he hadn't before experienced came at him, without blotting out the day, which was almost over. He would have liked to have slept then, but sleep, too, seemed beyond his reach.

At last, he took out his mobile and switched it on: there were several emails, most of them junk, and just a few text messages. Nothing from her. From his brother, his best man, there was one missed call and a text: *Your better off without that French hoor.*

Cathal made an effort to reply then read over what he'd written and deleted it, and turned his mobile off again.

After a while, he put his head down on the cushions, which felt soft, and let his mind fall into a series of difficult thoughts, which he laboured over. At one point, something from years ago came back to him: his mother standing at the gas cooker, making buttermilk pancakes, turning them on the pan. His father was at the head of the table, with himself and his brother seated on either side. Both were in their twenties at that time, in college, and had gone home for the weekend, with their laundry. His mother had served everyone, brought their plates to the table, and they had begun to eat. When she went to sit down, with her own plate, his brother had reached out and quickly pulled the chair from under her – and she had fallen backwards, onto the floor. She must have been near sixty years of age at that time, as she had married late, but his father had laughed – all three of them had laughed, heartily, and had kept on laughing while she picked the pancakes and the pieces of the broken plate up, off the floor.

If a part of Cathal now wondered how he might have turned out if his father had been another type of man and had not laughed, Cathal did not let his mind dwell on it. He told himself it meant little, that it was just a bad joke. When he no longer felt able or inclined to think over or consider anything more, he turned on his side, but at least another hour must have passed before sleep finally reached out and he felt himself falling into its relief, and a new darkness.

When he woke, it was past midnight. The TV was still going: some poker tournament with men in baseball caps and dark glasses, guarding their cards. For a while he sat watching these near-silent men placing and hedging their bets, and bluffing. Most lost and kept losing, or folded before they lost more. For another while, he watched with little interest, then he turned the TV off and sat listening to the quiet of the house, and realised Mathilde was there on the armchair, purring. He reached for her, lifted her into his arms. She weighed far more than he'd expected her to weigh and he put her out the back, watched her going off through the hedge, and locked the door.

By now, they would have had their first dance and might still have been dancing, into the early hours, at the Arklow Bay Hotel. He had paid for trays of snacks to be served with tea at 11 p.m.: several types of sandwiches, cocktail sausages, and mini vol-au-vents that would, by now, have been served and eaten by those with whom they might, in one way or another, have spent their lives. It was money he would never again see. A part of his mind hovered half-stupidly over these unwelcome facts while he stared at the empty champagne bottle on the floor, realising he probably wasn't sober. He thought of those cherries and how she had halved and stoned them that evening he'd asked her to marry him and how she'd made the tart, and what his going over their cost, that six euros, had cost him. Then he thought of that clafoutis, and how it had turned out to be burnt at the edges and half-raw in the centre – and a strange, almost comical noise came from somewhere down inside; didn't they say that a woman in love burned your dinner and that when she no longer cared she served it up half-raw?

When Cathal pulled the curtains, the window was wide open. The inflated castle was still out there – he could see it clearly under the street light – but there were no children now.

'Cunt,' he said.

Although he couldn't accurately attach this word to what she was, it was something he could say, something he could call her.

He stood in the quiet for a minute or two then heard a noise and realised a wasp had come in, and was flying about, zigzagging and bumping against and touching things in his sitting room. He took one of his unpolished shoes up off the floor and turned the overhead light on and found himself going after it, following its haphazard, unpredictable motions. A current of excited anger was rising up through his blood and, at one point, when he was standing on the arm of the sofa to reach, unsuccessfully, for it, he thought of Monika, that foreign cleaner on the stairs, and how she'd watched him as he'd passed on what should have been his wedding day; and of Cynthia, and how she had smiled that morning and how she had taken Sabine off unbeknownst to him, to the Shelbourne Hotel.

'Fucking cunts.' It sounded better when he added the other cunts, stronger.

He kept after the wasp, making bigger, braver swipes until it flew back to the window to get away from him and he had it cornered between the pane and sill, and killed it.

After he'd thrown the dead wasp out and closed the window, he felt a bit cooler and used the downstairs toilet to take a long piss. There was some triumph in doing this without having to lift the lid, without having to put the lid back down and having to wash his hands or making a pretence of having washed his hands afterwards – but the pleasure quickly vanished, and he then had to make himself climb the stairs.

As he climbed, he felt himself holding on to the banister, realising he was pulling himself along, woodenly, up the steps. He knew he could not blame the champagne but nonetheless found himself blaming it. Then a line from something he'd read somewhere came to him, to do with endings: about how, if things have not ended badly, that they have not ended.

When he reached the bedroom and unbuttoned his shirt and had taken his trousers off and lain down, he did not want to close his eyes; when he closed his eyes he could see more clearly the white cuff of his wedding shirt poking out through the wardrobe door, the stack of unopened, congratulatory cards and letters on the hallstand, the wedding dress she had insisted on showing him, the sons he would never have, and the non-refundable, diamond ring, which he couldn't return, shining inside its box on the bedside table, and could hear her saying, yet again, and very clearly, and so late in the day, that she'd changed her mind and had no wish to marry him after all.

Acknowledgements

The author would like to thank Felicity Blunt, Sophie Baker, Alex Bowler, Aisling Brennan, Silvia Crompton, Noreen Doody, Katie Harrison, Niall MacMonagle, Rosie Pierce, Sheila Purdy, Katie Raissian, Ciara Roche and Josephine Salverda. And her French publisher, Sabine Wespieser, who first published this text as a standalone story under the title *Misogynie*.